In memory of my Sita Pati, so sweet and so strong
RL

For my mom, who has gone and come back many times
SP

First edition 2022. Library of Congress Catalog Card Number pending. ISBN 978-1-5362-0717-0.
This book was typeset in Trebuchet. The illustrations were done in gouache and acrylic and assembled digitally.
Candlewick Press, 99 Dover Street, Somerville, Massachusetts 02144. www.candlewick.com.
Printed in Humen, Dongguan, China. 21 22 23 24 25 26 APS 10 9 8 7 6 5 4 3 2 1

I'll Go and Come Back

Rajani LaRocca   illustrated by Sara Palacios

CANDLEWICK PRESS

For the first time since I was a baby, I flew across the world to see
aunties and uncles, cousin-brothers and cousin-sisters, and Sita Pati.

But India was so different from home.

The sky thundered and poured through the humid air. Mosquitoes whined when I tried to sleep. Street dogs woke me at dawn. Trucks honked and children chattered and neighbors gossiped on crowded roads. Everyone stared.

In the morning and evening, the house was packed with relatives and friends.

But during the day, with my cousins at school, I was lonely.

I wanted to go home.

Then Sita Pati called me: "Jyoti, va, ma."

She didn't speak much English, and I didn't speak much Tamil, but we understood each other.

"Bath?" she asked. "Teeth?"

"All finished," I said. And then I tried the Tamil: "Yella aachi."

She laughed and took my hand.

"Rangoli," said Sita Pati.

We made designs in the courtyard with colored sand—bright pink and sparkling blue and dazzling gold.

She dressed me in the same colors and tucked strands of jasmine in my hair.

She took me to the market. I'd never seen so many types of vegetables! One looked like it could slither away.

"Padaval," said Sita Pati. "Snake gourd."

"Let's get okra instead," I said.

At home, we played a game called Pallanguzhi.
Sometimes Pati counted wrong. She liked to win.

Sita Pati made chapatis, hot-hot, and flipped them with bare fingers.
I ate one with spicy okra and cool yogurt rice.

We spent our days playing and reading and
cooking. At night, we sipped warm milk with
saffron to bring us sweet dreams.

When it was time to go home, I didn't want to. I held Pati's hand with its soft, soft skin. Her sari rustled and smelled of silk. "Goodbye," I said.

"Poitu variya?" asked Sita Pati. "Will you go and come?"

And I remembered that no one in India just said "goodbye." "I'll go and come back," I said. "Poitu varen."

The next summer, Sita Pati flew across the world to visit us in America. She seemed smaller than I remembered.

The sun blazed and the air conditioner droned. The streets stayed empty and silent. Pati told my mom she couldn't hear so much as a sparrow chirp from inside the house.

Pati looked lonely. I wondered if she wanted to go home.

I still didn't speak much Tamil and she still didn't speak much English, but we understood each other.

"Bath?" I asked. "Teeth?"

"Yella aachi," she said. She'd remembered to put them in. I laughed and took her hand.

"Hopscotch," I said.

We drew on the sidewalk with chalk—bright pink and cool blue and sunny yellow.

I dressed Pati in the same colors.

We shopped at the grocery store. She'd never seen so many types of bread!

"Chapati?" asked Pati.

"Tortilla," I said.

We played a game called Chutes and Ladders. Pati still liked to win.
So did I. But I counted right . . . most of the time.

We made hot-hot quesadillas. I ate them with salsa, and Pati chose coconut chutney.

We spent our days playing and reading and cooking. At night, we sipped hot cocoa to bring us sweet dreams.

When it was time for Pati to go home, I didn't want her to.
Pati said, "Poitu varen," and then, "I'll go and come back."
Her skin was soft as ever.

Pati flew back home to India, but our love stretched across the world.

And we both remembered . . .

our promises to come back.